North Pole East

Santa's New Town

PAULA STONEBACK

Paula Stoneback

Illustrated by Parker Simpson

Junior Illustrator Julea Foley

Cover design and illustrated by Parker Simpson
Three images in chapter 6 illustrated by Julea Foley

ISBN 978-1-7325072-0-3

For Deb
My Inspiration

"Look, Mom, look! Here's a sign that Santa put up, announcing that we all need to be at the town meeting tomorrow night!" exclaimed Ezekiel, the elf. "The other elves were talking about it in our last day of school today." As his mother looked ever-so lovingly at her son, she too had heard rumors that big news was in the air. The entire town was excited to hear what Santa had to say. They had not had a town meeting in over a month which was very unusual for the North Pole, a city filled with fun and laughter as it prepared for the biggest day of the year.

Ezekiel, or EZE, as all of his friends called him, was thrilled that his schooling was finished, and he could now be a helping hand in Santa's organization. Every elf had to go to school for five years at the Elf State Academy, so they could learn everything there was to know in the world. Now it was his time to decide what he wanted to do with all of that amazing knowledge. EZE loved wearing his purple hat and purple shoes for the past five years, but he was now ready to wear the typical elf colors of red and green. Usually by the last day of school, every elf knew what he or she wanted to do. *Hmmm...do I want to make toys for all of the wonderful children, work in the craft shop making exquisite gifts for Santa's craft store, help to run the cafeteria making the amazing food for the town, manage the mailroom where all of the kids' letters arrive, or handle the town's decorations and lights. I could also maintain Santa's sleigh and the city train that takes everybody around the town, or last, but not least, I could take care of Santa's reindeer in the reindeer barn.* EZE struggled with these thoughts throughout his entire five years at the Elf State Academy. Each job was so important in helping to make Christmas special for every child and even the parents of the children, so it was a huge decision.

EZE, who had bushy red hair with a freckled complexion, got along with everybody. He was very easy-going which is how he earned his nickname. His name fit him perfectly. He enjoyed listening to music and sometimes played the drums. His favorite fun thing to do was to play soccer with the other elves. He had some great skills and could score a lot of goals. All of his pals loved to hang around with him.

"What does your friend, Lucas, want to do? Has he told you?" asked EZE's mom, Lilly.

EZE thought about it for a second, and replied, "Mom, this is going to sound very strange, but most of my friends have not decided what they want to do either. All of our teachers told us not to worry, that it would come to us in time. I sure hope so!" Being the great mother that she was, she told EZE not to think about it as well. Secretly she was wondering what was going on. All of her elf friends knew by their fourth year of school where they wanted to work.

Lilly had always wanted to design and create new vases for Santa's craft store. She could make anything out of glass but mainly concentrated on crafting elegant vases with flared rims in fanciful colors. All of the other elves oohed and aahed every time she came up with a new design. She just knew she had to be a glassblower. Every thought that entered her head was all about making pretty vases for Santa's guests to admire. Her new vases sold out in record time every time she presented her latest. She was so proud to earn money to help pay for the North Pole's expenses. Yes, even the North Pole had bills!

"Well, maybe Santa will have some ideas for you. We can talk to him after the town meeting tomorrow. He knows everything!" Lilly tried to reassure EZE as they headed to the cafeteria to enjoy a scrumptious meal made by many of her closest elf friends. "Let's see what tomorrow brings!"

Chapter 2 - Ezekiel and His Friends

As the day unfolded, EZE decided to meet up with Lucas, Emily, and Zack, who were three of his constant companions and classmates. "Hey, let's go visit Rudolph and see if we can talk to him about the town meeting tonight. He's sure to know something, don't you think?" EZE questioned excitedly, thinking he had to be on a hot trail.

Emily chimed in, "Yes, he's usually in the know. Santa includes him in everything."

Lucas yelled, "Well, sure, after what happened to him a long time ago, Santa doesn't ever want him to be left out again!"

Zack, the quietest of the elves spoke up, and said, "Rudolph has been an inspiration to the world so no matter what, we can at least talk to him and see if he thinks there is something good we can do for Santa's organization."

EZE agreed, stating, "Ok, that sounds like a plan! Off to see Rudolph in the barn!"

Rudolph had so many friends that it was sometimes difficult to get to visit with him alone, but EZE, Lucas, Emily and Zack were sure they could steal some time with him as they headed over to the reindeer barn. If Rudolph was too busy, they would talk to Donner or Blitzen until Rudolph had a minute. Donner was the coolest of all of the reindeer, always wearing sunglasses and had the most interesting stories to tell. Blitzen could usually read minds. For some reason, he had a special talent that Santa gave to him. Blitzen was the reindeer everybody counted on for help and advice when they needed it. He always made each elf feel very special.

When they came into the barn, Rudolph was singing songs with Comet and Cupid. Vixen was playing the piano, and Dasher was playing the snare drums. Of course, Dancer and Prancer were doing what they did best, dancing and prancing around, showing off their incredible dance moves. "If only the rest of us could dance like them!" yelled Lucas. The reindeer were happy to see the elves and invited them to sing along, and it was quite a song they all belted out. "Rudolph, The Red-Nosed Reindeer", was their favorite song, but this time they were singing, "It's Beginning to Look a Lot Like Christmas". *Good enough to be a band*, they all thought! *It was just so much fun to be an elf*, thought EZE.

Blitzen, who was sitting at the table nearby, enjoying the show, looked at EZE, and whispered, "It's so much fun to be a reindeer too!"

A lot of laughing occurred when the song was over because every day was like Christmas in the North Pole, not just beginning to 'look' like Christmas! They couldn't imagine what it would be like where every day wasn't looking like Christmas. When it quieted down, EZE asked Rudolph if he had a moment to talk with them. The happy, little reindeer's red nose lit up in excitement and responded, "Absolutely, I always have time for you! Come, sit down, and let's talk."

The reindeer barn had a huge wooden table that they all sat around whenever they had meetings, when Santa came to talk with them, and just in general, when they were eating their reindeer food. They loved their place where they lived. Santa always took very good care of them. Rudolph sat down at the table, and asked the elves what was going on.

"Rudolph, do you know what tonight's town meeting is all about? Have you heard?" EZE eagerly questioned him.

Rudolph was wondering if this is why the elves came over and said softly, "Santa has been really secretive about what is going on, but he is supposed to meet with all of us reindeer five minutes before the meeting to clue us in. So we will know a little bit then, but we suppose we will find out right when you do. I am very excited though as I just feel like wonderful news is coming!"

Lucas responded, "I'm wondering if Santa is getting a new sleigh with more bells and whistles for this Christmas?"

Again Rudolph said, "That would be nice, but the one we have is awesome as it is. Let's just wait and see. It won't be long, my friends. Now run along and eat your dinner. See you at the meeting tonight!"

Chapter 3 - The Town Meeting

All of lights were aglow on Santa's stage, and music was playing as the elves filed into the meeting. Elves were known to be extremely orderly, so it didn't take long until everybody was situated and ready for the news! Ol' St. Nick was always on time too, so when he said 7:00 for the town meeting, they all knew he would be talking before 7:01.

"Hello, everybody! How are you all doing? I'm sorry it's been a lot longer than normal since I've called you to the town center. Mrs. Claus and I have been working hard this past year and have some very exciting news to tell all of you!" The elves clapped nervously, waiting with excitement.

"I know you have always supported me with my ideas, and this is news of a dramatic change in our lives. I hope you will be as happy as I think you will be after tonight! I have three big announcements to tell you.

As you know, we are at capacity in the North Pole and running out of room for our operations. We have grown and grown so big in order to fulfill all of the kids' wishes and have run out of space. So, we are not only going to expand, we are relocating to the North Pole East in two weeks." Everybody looked around in a state of curiosity and confusion, not knowing where the North Pole East was. Santa continued, "Many of you are wondering where this place is. It's really just to the east side of town, and it's over 100 acres of land that has been donated to us by the Gerkin family. They knew we needed more room, and they have never used the territory and thought it would be wonderful for all of us! We will have new facilities for everybody. I can't wait to tell you all about it!"

EZE looked over at his mom, and asked her what she thought. "You know how smart Santa is, so it must be a good thing. No worries, it will be wonderful," she said nervously. "Shhhh. Santa looks like he's going to say more!"

"As I said, that's not all of the news that I have for you. I have an even bigger announcement! I have been working with the Crofton Computer Company to develop an amazing computer system that will take us into the 21st century. It will be a super computer that will monitor everything to make sure that all children are accounted for, that every child receives the present he or she wants, and that my sleigh will be faster and more efficient when the big day arrives. We have a little more than two months to make sure that everything will run smoothly on Christmas Eve through Christmas morning. I will share other news about the new computer system; like a web site for our craft shop, a new food-ordering system for the cafeteria, an email-system for the mailroom, a super-duper new train, and so many other things that are extremely exciting!

And as for the third announcement, I will let Mrs. Claus tell all of you," Santa said excitedly as he looked out at the anxious crowd.

The entire town loved to listen to Mrs. Claus when she spoke too. She always had a smile on her face. She was in charge of the Elf State Academy, so everyone knew when she spoke it was usually about the direction of the academy. "Hello, my precious ones. I wanted to share with you that our newest graduating elves are going to run the computer department in the North Pole East! Now, don't you worry, my graduates. You will be given two weeks of training and will know everything that you need to know about computers. I know how intelligent you all are, so this will be a snap for you. Santa and I have been planning for this day for the past year. We figured your class would run this department, so that's why none of you knew what you wanted to do." EZE looked around at his classmates and saw the look of relief, the same feeling he had as well. He had no idea that they all had felt nervous about their future.

"You couldn't decide what you wanted to do because you didn't know about the computer system. Now that you know about it, you will realize you were made for this job! I know you can do fabulous work making this all happen," she said confidently.

Santa chimed in, "Welcome to our working world, my elves!" The entire town erupted with cheering and clapping. Mother Lilly gazed at her Ezekiel with so much admiration that she thought her heart was going to burst! What an exciting opportunity for her son!

Santa called for order and told them all to have a wonderful evening and that he would meet up with the computer elves first thing in the morning. Their world would be changing soon, and they would all learn about the new events in the upcoming days.

As they all headed hastily to their homes, the excitement was overwhelming for EZE. He wondered if he was even going to be able to sleep, waiting for the next morning to arrive. He just knew this was going to be the beginning of the best life he could ever imagine! As he laid his head on his pillow, he drifted to sleep, dreaming of what the next day would bring.

Chapter 4 - Santa Meets With the Graduates

"Good morning, my little elves! How are things going?" asked their wonderful, jolly leader in his beautiful red suit and black boots. EZE and his friends all greeted Santa with extreme happiness, knowing that he was entrusting them with the future of Christmas!

"Today begins a new day for the North Pole, um, excuse me, I should start saying the North Pole East from this point forward. I have to take a step back and tell you why I agreed to make all of this happen and go forward with such a dramatic change for all of us.

There have been a few children that have been missed in the past Christmases. From time to time, children travel to relatives' homes, or they are in the hospital, or they are even homeless; and I have to know where they are at all times to be able to be there for them. Christmas is most of the kids' favorite day of the year, and they are waiting all year for this day to arrive. The children have to be able to reach me to let me know where they are for this special day. I cannot stress enough that I must not miss one single child. It is simply that important to me, and I know that you are aware of that as well.

I'm sure that most of you know about computers and how people use them. They send emails, call on cell phones and use web sites; so we have to change and grow with the world to co-exist in the same manner. We are setting up a web site for all of the people who can't make it to the North Pole to be able to see everything in the craft shop, and we will set up a camera for the children to see what the reindeer and all of my elves are doing to get ready for their special day! The children can also send emails to me. They always have lots of questions for me. Like, 'Santa, what if I don't have a chimney? How will you get into my house?' and 'How do you eat all of the cookies that so many kids leave for you?' and 'What are the reindeer's favorite cookies?' are just a few of the many questions. I want to reassure and ease their minds about many of their worries.

You will learn everything over these next two weeks so that we can go live by November 1st." EZE and his friends all looked at each other, nodding their heads in agreement that this was going to be a wonderful thing. Their smiles were from ear to ear. Technology was a good thing, and they were going to make sure Santa's vision was fulfilled. The North Pole East was sounding better and better every minute of the day!

Santa continued on, "Once we have everything in place in two weeks, we will start running virtual test runs that we can watch on the computers how the entire 24 hours will go on Christmas Eve. Sort of like a pretend Christmas Eve. This way we will make sure that all will run smoothly on the actual night for every child. Does that sound good?"

"That's fabulous, Santa!" all of the elves chanted and cheered at once.

EZE looked over at Emily and screeched, "I can't wait!!"

Emily replied, "I know, me too - it's amazing, and the kids are going to love it!"

Santa added, "One more thing. At the end of the two weeks, I will have your new hats and shoes to give you. I know you are excited to start your new journey making our organization even better!

The town train is waiting for all of you outside to take you over to the new computer facility in the North Pole East. I have gathered everything you will need from your homes to make your transition easy. Just look for your bags with your names on them. You will each have a room at the new place as well, and you will see where to go once you get there."

Santa wished them well for the next two weeks as he turned everything over to the Crofton Computer Company Chosen Crew to work with the lucky elves. The Chosen Crew was the expert training staff at the company, and Santa had to have the best for his team.

Chapter 5 - The Training, Week 1

As the days passed, EZE and his enlightened friends learned everything and then some about the largest central processor that ever existed. Circuits, memory, microchips, platform, networking, multiprocessing, web sites, gigabytes.....the learning was endless it seemed. Day after day, they learned everything about how the new computer system ran and how it worked in every area of Santa's organization.

The computer facility was most spacious, and each of the elves had his or her room with their names on the doors. It was truly a dream come true for each of the elves. Somehow they would understand and know it all in just two weeks if that is what Santa said. After all, Santa always knew best.

They learned all about the satellite screen that they could watch Santa on when he wanted to talk with them. They would also be able to watch how Christmas Eve was going to happen on the screen. It was the most amazing screen with so many options – they were excited about the possibilities of how they could use it.

"We sure are lucky to be elves," Lucas confided in EZE. "Once we learn something, it just stays in our brains, and we can access that knowledge any time we want!"

EZE agreed with Lucas wholeheartedly as he proclaimed, "This is going to be the best Christmas ever for the kids! I've learned so much already just in this first week. I never knew my brain could hold so much knowledge!" he giggled.

Just then, they heard Zack come bursting through the door, almost running everybody over. "Hey, guys! Santa just pulled up in his sleigh out front! He must be coming to see how we are doing." All of the elves quickly came to attention, and sure enough, Santa strode through the door. It was nice for them to see Santa in his dress downs.

Santa didn't always wear his red suits. Sometimes he was in his winter outfits which were much simpler - a cream-colored shirt with a soft, green jacket, jeans with a black belt and a shiny buckle, and loafers on his feet. *Always the shiny buckle*, thought EZE. His beautiful beard was always the same though, perfectly groomed.

"Good morning, my amazing computer elves! How are you doing? I have heard from the Chosen Crew that you are all doing incredibly well, and that everything is coming together nicely. It sure makes me proud of you to hear that you are all up to speed on things. I just wanted to stop by and tell you to keep up the great work. One more week to go, and this should be an even more exciting week to come as you will see how the whole virtual process will work. It is the most amazing process you will ever see! So, have a wonderful week learning." Santa waved to everybody as he left them all to continue learning. Off he went in that magnificent sleigh with Rudolph leading the way.

Chapter 6 - The Training, Week 2

The second week was upon the elves. They were watching short videos of every process of Santa's System, the name that was selected for the entire operation. From how the kids could write to Santa; how the computer logged those emails; how the computer kept the addresses for where the kids were going to be for Christmas; how the wish list went to the toy shop where the elves would build the toys and games; how the items were put in storage areas; how the items were loaded onto the sleighs; how Santa made all of the deliveries; and how Santa got back home after a wonderful night of making children happy. They did test run after test run and watched Santa's System play out.

There were a few glitches that were happening. Some of the lists of gifts would wind up at the wrong house, so the elves had to re-design that part of the system. The System was now in the elves' hands because they knew more than the Crofton Chosen Crew at this point. With their knowledge, it didn't take long. Elves were just incredibly intelligent. They knew they would be able to fix any bugs in the System. The Chosen Crew stayed around until the end of the week in case they were needed, but they knew the elves had everything under control.

Various bugs were happening throughout the week. The elves were beginning to wonder if something was wrong with their magnificent computer system. In the United States alone, there were numerous issues. Billy, from eastern Kansas, had wanted a race car track, but he wound up with a racing bike. Susie, from Phoenix, Arizona, wanted an Ipod, but she wound up with a doll.

One time, Santa had all of the wrong items in his sled for the whole town of Pasadena, California. That was the most disastrous thing and just could not happen. Sadie, from Anchorage, Alaska, asked for a new pair of boots, but the computer picked it up as a belt. So she was not a happy child on the virtual video. Charley, from Philadelphia, PA, emailed that he was on vacation at his uncle's house in Pittsburgh, but some of the emails were getting lost in the shuffle; and Santa did not know where Charley was on Christmas morning when Santa showed up in Philadelphia. As you can imagine, these types of things had to be fixed immediately, or the children and Santa would not be happy. The elves had one mission - to make it all happen perfectly!

After three days of working out the issues, it appeared that all was working well! The System was ready for everybody else to watch and learn what the elves had been doing for the past two weeks. On Sunday the whole town was moving over to all of the new facilities in The North Pole East. Surely, a grand time was ahead for all of them.

Chapter 7 - The Move to North Pole East

Today was the big day. All of the computer elves waited anxiously for their families to arrive and see their new home. Santa presented all of the computer elves with their shiny red and green hats and shoes, so they were going to surprise their families with their new outfits.

Santa had made everything so perfect for the whole town. Rudolph and all of his reindeer friends were playing music and dancing when the train pulled up with all of the excited elves. It was a wonderful welcome. Of course, the town maintenance elves had already been provided the plans of getting the town up to snuff. Trees needed to be decorated, lights needed to be hung, and pretty bows needed to be placed on all of the lampposts. They were ready to roll with that. Fancy, new train tracks were placed all over the town, so the ride was as smooth as anybody could imagine.

When Lilly saw the new craft store with the amazing sign on the building, reading "SANTA'S GIFT SHOPPE", her eyes lit up with an animated glow. She couldn't believe it! "Wowza," was all she could breathe across her lips. She looked over at the other crafters to see tears in their eyes as well.

"Santa gave us a name on our shop. That is terrific!" Jimmy, the box maker, yelled to the others. "And to know that all the people will be able to see what we make on a website is unbelievable. I just can't wait to make more wooden boxes that they love. I hear there will be an unlimited supply of wood for me. Oh, yeah…Oh, yeah," Jimmy shouted to all who could hear him.

The others were excited as well. The post office team saw their building called "SANTA'S MAIL AND EMAIL CENTER". The cafeteria team was delighted to see the enormous building that must be theirs, called "SANTA'S CAFE AND EATERY". They heard there was a whole separate bakery area where they could make
their yummy kiffles, fruit cakes, cheesecakes, and decorated cookies.

Santa had really made them all feel very special as they were beginning their new journey in the North Pole East.

Dasher, Dancer, Prancer, Vixen, Comet, Cupid, Donner, Blitzen and Rudolph loved their new barn, "SANTA'S REINDEER BARN", and they couldn't wait for all of the elves to come visit them to see their new area. And to think that cameras would be rolling in the barn so the kids could watch what they were doing during the days. They weren't sure if they were going to bore the kids or not because they usually ate, drank, and slept through most days. They did sing and dance fairly often, so they knew the kids would love that. Throughout the year, they occasionally pulled Santa in his sleigh to pick up some of Santa's guests and bring them back to the North Pole, but they weren't sure if that was going to be on video or not.

There was a huge building dedicated for the elves to make the toys and games that the kids wanted for their gifts. Santa came up with a really great name on their building which was "SANTA'S MAKE-A-WISH TOY SHOPPE". This facility took up about 50 acres of the entire town. They had more space to spread out and really build some fabulous gifts for the children. There would be no stopping them this year.

The elves spent a few hours learning their way around on the train through the facilities. They knew Santa would be coming to talk with each of them as the day progressed. After all, he always took great care of them. They were also anxious to see what the computer elves had been up to.

Chapter 8 - The Virtual Test Runs

The happy elves had been working away for weeks in their new space. They were turning out work like they couldn't believe. They were able to work faster and more efficiently because of the new computer system. Lilly was creating a new vase every day, one prettier than the next. She knew the demand on the website was going to exceed her wildest dreams. To think that her vases would be in so many homes gave her a very warm feeling in her heart.

Each department had been working hand in hand with the computer elves to make sure they knew exactly how to do everything using Santa's System. Everything was going very smoothly. Letters and emails were pouring in, children were talking with Santa online, people were ordering items from the Craft Shoppe and the elves were shipping them out as fast as they could. It was a seamless operation. Santa and Mrs. Claus were wondering why they didn't do this a few years back, but they realized they weren't ready for all of this new technology until now.

The cafeteria was a wonderful place to eat. The elves could go there for all of their delicious meals. They could go on the computer and order their food ahead of time if they knew what they wanted. The choices were endless. They needed to keep their energy up as they had much work to do for Santa and the children!

Santa came around to each facility to talk with the elves and to show them how their part contributed to the whole System. Every segment was so important, and Santa showed each group of elves a virtual show of how Christmas Eve would go. They all knew they were the most important team that ever existed.

The elves were able to see Santa talk to the children as well. Santa told the kids about his magical key to get into the houses that didn't have chimneys. Some chimneys were too small for him anyway so he used the key at those houses too.

From all of the cookies that the kids left for him, he also had to figure out a plan what to do with all of those cookies; or he wasn't going to fit in any chimney if he kept eating all of them! He told the kids that he would eat one cookie, give some to the reindeer and then box up the rest to bring back for National Elf Cookie Day. "What is National Elf Cookie Day?" some of them asked Santa. "It's the day after Christmas that all of the elves sit down and eat the cookies. After all, the elves had done so much to make Christmas perfect for everybody, so I wanted to share the cookies with them! It is the day we all celebrate after a wonderful Christmas was had by the children! Oh, and don't worry what kind of cookies the reindeer like. They find plenty that they love; although, Rudolph certainly enjoys chocolate-chip cookies more than the other reindeer do!"

For the first three weeks, every virtual test went smoothly. All children were accounted for, all children received the right presents in the right place, and Santa arrived back home safely after a successful night. It was one smooth operation they had created. OR SO THEY THOUGHT.....

Chapter 9 - Hector "The Hack" Gerkin

"HO,HO,HO is going to be HA,HA,HA when I get finished with Santa and his silly team of elves," snarled Hector Gerkin in an evil manner. "Just who do they think they are, living in the North Pole East like they are kings and queens?" His dog, Madison, looked up at him wondering why he was up to no good. She was hoping he wouldn't do anything bad because it was lonely when he was gone for a year in Time-Out Town for hacking into the government's computer. She didn't want him to ever do that again.

"Don't worry, Madison. You and I will show them who we are," he growled. Madison whimpered and then went to lay down with hopes that Hector would behave. Madison loved to look at Hector. He had a perfect head of brown hair, green eyes, and usually a happy smile on his face when he looked at her. She always heard how intelligent he was when it came to computers. She just hoped he could stay on a good path with his knowledge.

Hector found a way to get into Santa's System and caused some glitches for the computer elves. He just laughed and laughed when Sadie got a belt instead of those boots she wanted, and Billy got the bike instead of a race car set. "Do they think that just happened by accident?! They don't know who they are messing with. Just wait until Christmas Eve! I do give them credit though as they keep fixing the issues pretty fast. I have a new plan though, and they will have no clue!"

This time Hector had discovered that he could put a virus in the System that would allow the computer to be good for one day, then a disaster would happen the next day, then a good day after that, and then disaster again. It would really make the elves go crazy with what was happening. "Those little elf brains will be mush by the time I'm finished," he laughed deliriously.

Hector thought back to the Christmas when he was younger when Santa forgot about him. He was in the hospital sick over Christmas, and Santa never showed up. He just assumed Santa knew where he was, and he had never forgiven Santa even though the following year Santa gave him twice the amount of gifts that he had asked for. What he didn't know is that Santa dropped the gifts off at his house, and his parents decided to give his gifts to a neighbor child whose parents didn't have much money. His parents figured Hector was in the hospital, so he wouldn't miss the train set that he had wanted.

Hector began getting in trouble over the years after that Christmas because he was angry and bitter. He hacked into people's computers and infected the computers so badly that they wouldn't work. He had a good computer job for a while, making a lot of money. But then he went too far one year when he hacked into the government's computer, and it didn't take them long to figure out it was him. While he was in Time-Out Town, a doctor would come to visit him every week to help him with his problems. The doctor was able to get Hector feeling better and to stop being angry. Hector had been good for many years until he got the crippling news of what his uncle did.

Chapter 10 - The Gerkin's Donation

Jasper Gerkin, an elegant man with silver hair, was an accountant his whole life. He had inherited the North Pole East from his grandparents when he was younger. His family had owned this land for many years. He didn't really know what to do with the land anymore. At one point, he considered developing it into a resort area, but he knew that was not his calling. When he heard that Santa was running out of room in the North Pole, he thought, *What better way could there be to represent our family name by donating the land to Santa and his organization?* The only relative he had was his nephew, Hector, but Hector was involved in computers and was always getting in trouble so no sense giving it to him. He was sure Hector wouldn't want to be bothered with the land anyway.

When Jasper met with Mr. and Mrs. Santa Claus a year ago to offer them the land, they were overwhelmed with Jasper's generosity. What an enormous offer, and Santa and Mrs. Claus knew they would be eternally grateful. They accepted graciously and told him they would take very good care of this gift he was giving to them. "We will definitely let everybody know about your family and what a wonderful thing you are doing. We want to name one of our new buildings after you as well," Santa said.

Jasper replied, "Thank you, but that is really not necessary. I just want to know it is in good hands and there's no better cause than your organization as you do everything for the children. It will be wonderful for everybody!"

Agreeing wholeheartedly, Santa said, "We will announce it to the town next year once everything is in place and ready for them. I want it to be perfect before they know about it."

Jasper understood and excitedly said, "It will be our secret then!"

Hector had recently gotten wind of what his uncle did, and it threw him for a loop. He thought for sure that his uncle was going to pass the land to him when it was time. *Why on earth would he give it to Santa and his organization?* he thought. *Just another thing to make me angry about Santa! They already have the North Pole. I wish I would have talked more with my uncle about my plans!*

Hector had wanted to start a new computer company and open up shop in the North Pole East, providing security to companies so that hackers can't get in and ruin their work. From being such a great hacker himself, he knew how to protect companies and figured it would make him a millionaire. Oh, the plans he had!!! Well, those plans sure were spoiled, so Hector only knew one thing to do.

He would become a pest to Santa's System, and maybe Santa would think that they would need to leave the North Pole East and return the land to the family. At that point, Uncle Jasper would surely give him the land once Hector told him what he wanted to do with it. "They will think they have no choice but to leave!! And finally a Gerkin will put this land to good use!"

Chapter 11 - The Virus

The next two weeks sure were crazy for the computer elves. "What is happening?" asked EZE to all of his confidants. We've watched the virtual shows, and they seem to be good one day, bad the next.

"How can we fix this when it seems like it is good the next day?" wondered Emily. Lucas, Zack, and all of the other elves agreed that it was the strangest thing they had come across.

EZE told his group that he would go talk to Blitzen to see if he could come up with any ideas. "Maybe there is something going on that we might not be thinking of," he said as he walked out of the computer center and headed over to SANTA'S REINDEER BARN.

"Hey, Blitzen! Your place is magnificent! I will have to come back when I can spend more time to check everything out! I was hoping to talk with you a few minutes if you are game?" EZE politely asked Blitzen.

"Sure thing. What is happening, my friend?" asked Blitzen.

EZE proceeded to tell Blitzen the whole story from start to finish about all of the strange things that were happening with the computer. EZE was very troubled because Christmas was less than a month away, and they had to figure this out to be sure Christmas Eve was going to happen without any glitches.

Blitzen listened and listened until he finally spoke. "Well, EZE, it appears to me that it may be a force outside of the computer making this happen. It doesn't sound like it could be the computer after all the hard work you and the other elves did to make this whole thing work," Blitzen suggested.

EZE looked stunned, realizing that he had only been focusing his thoughts on what is wrong with the computer processor. He should have had faith that this computer system wouldn't let them down. *It must be what they call a hacker*, EZE thought. EZE had heard of hackers, but he knew nobody would want to interfere with Santa's System. "You are so right, Blitzen! Thank you for opening my eyes. You are a genius! I do believe we need to find what they call a hacker. It should be easy, and we will let Santa know. Thanks for your help, as always!"

EZE ran back to his center to share the good news with his team. They were all in agreement when they heard what Blitzen had suggested to EZE, so now they knew they had a mission to find who was doing this. "Let's run the tests we have to figure this out," EZE exclaimed. "It shouldn't take long to find the hacker."

They knew every computer in the world had what was called an IP address. An IP address was a long number that was assigned to every computer out there, and it was printed on the back of each computer. Once they could see which computer was hacking into the System, they would know who this pesty person was and where they lived. Then they could find the source and shut it down. Stranger than ever though, when they saw where the virus was coming from, it scrambled the IP address into five different IP addresses. This just didn't make sense. Somehow this hacker had figured out a way to throw everybody off course if anybody was looking for him.

"Could this be something smarter than we realize?" asked Lucas, feeling a little scared about the answer.

"How else can we figure this out? Let's do a search and see if anybody ever put out any bad publicity about Santa or the North Pole. I can't imagine that happening, but let's cover all of our bases," added Emily.

Much to their shocking surprise, there were a couple of ads out on the internet from years back of somebody badmouthing Christmas and Santa Claus. "Let's run the IP address of where those ads came from," suggested Zack.

"Good idea," agreed EZE, as they all sat down to do the search.

When the IP address came up, and it flashed across the screen with the name of the person who owned the computer, they all sat in disbelief. "Wow, who wants to break this news to Santa? I just can't believe it," shouted Emily.

Chapter 12 – The Surprise

EZE started off hesitantly as he said, "Santa, we have some surprising news to tell you! We now know that we have a computer hacker who has unleashed a virus in our computer system which is the reason some days aren't going so well in the test runs. We believe we know what computer is doing the damage to the System."

"Who or what do you believe is doing this?" Santa asked anxiously.

EZE continued, "This computer is at Jasper Gerkin's home. We were all shocked as he is the one who donated all of this land to us. Do you have any idea why he would do such a bad thing?"

Santa looked ashamed for some reason, and the elves all got a curious look on their faces. "What's wrong, Santa?" they all asked.

"My sweet, intelligent elves, I believe you have stumbled on to something else. It's not Jasper. He would never do that. But now you have me believing that it is his nephew, Hector Gerkin. He was one of the boys that I didn't know was in the hospital one year, so I took his gifts to his house. His parents told me he was in the hospital later and that they had given his presents to a neighbor child. Hector was angry when he got out the hospital and wrote a letter telling me so. I told him I was sorry, and he said later that he was fine and would get over it. I thought everything was ok, but this was one of the reasons why I started the whole computer system. I feel so badly when something like this happens, and I don't want it to happen again. I asked his uncle Jasper how Hector was doing when Mrs. Claus and I met with him, and Jasper said Hector was doing great in the computer world. Jasper said Hector was very intelligent but wished Hector would have made wiser decisions. He had gotten himself in trouble from time to time. I will drop by and talk to Hector in the morning. Thank you for your infinite knowledge! Have a good night and know this will all be ok tomorrow," Santa reassured all of them.

Chapter 13 - Santa Meets with Hector

As Santa landed his sleigh in front of Hector's beautiful home, he told all of the reindeer to sit tight as he might be talking to Hector for a while. Just then, the front door of the house flew open, and Hector came walking out with his sidekick, Madison. Madison started barking which made Hector look up to a shocking surprise: Santa was walking right towards him! Hector's knees started to buckle as he didn't know what to do. Santa had never come to his new home before, but he never really had a reason to before now. He knew why Santa was there. Madison quieted down when she realized it was Santa and ran right up to him. Santa patted her on her head with his soft, white gloves which made Madison know everything was going to be ok.

"Hello, Hector. Sorry to surprise you, but I didn't think you would be here if I called ahead and asked to speak with you," proclaimed Santa. "I need to understand why you are hacking into our System."

Hector lowered his head in shame and said, "I didn't think you would find me so quickly, but I guess with your incredible, new computer system and your most intelligent elves, I should have figured you would be able to track this back to me. It is quite the dream computer system, I must admit," he confided in Santa.

Santa proceeded with a big smile, "Thank you. I had to have the best because I don't want any kids to be missed on Christmas like you thought you were missed. Your parents apologized to me, but they were just trying to help the neighbors."

"Wait, what do you mean, my parents apologized?" Hector asked in disbelief as he felt a lump in his throat.

"They wrote to me what happened when you were in the hospital - they thought you would be okay with them giving your presents to the neighbor boy whose family didn't have much money. They said you were good friends with him and would be pleased to make your friend, Joshua, happy. Are you saying they never told you? I'm so sorry if that happened," said Santa.

Hector was devastated. All these years he was angry with Santa, and only to find out his parents were just doing a good thing. "They never told me," Hector said apologetically. "I'm so sorry I was angry with you and wrote you that mean letter. Please forgive me, Santa!"

"That is okay, I accept your apology. Now, I have an offer for you that I hope you will accept," Santa stated.

"I would like you to come run our security department for our computer system. You are obviously one of the best hackers there is, so I figure you would be the best person to run this department to keep us safe in the future. My elves were quite impressed with the intricate virus that you created, so I'm hoping to put that great knowledge to good use by putting you in charge. I know they would be happy to have you on our side. What do you say?" asked Santa. Hector thought he was having a dream and couldn't quite respond to Santa. Santa continued, "You will have your own place there, and the building will be appropriately named to honor your family. Madison will, of course, have her own bed and playroom. She will probably love the elves and the reindeer. What do you think, Hector?"

Hector gathered himself and was as honored as he's ever been. Madison nudged him gently to please say, "YES!" He finally could speak, "Why, Santa, I accept your offer, and I promise that I will offer the best security you could imagine! Thank you for having faith in me. I will report for duty first thing in the morning!" He turned to Madison and said, "Come along, Madison, we have some packing to do!"

As Santa pulled away with his reindeer, Rudolph lit the way with his shiny, red nose. Santa had a wonderful thought...*My team was now complete.*

Chapter 14 - Two Weeks and Counting

With just two weeks remaining before Christmas, everything was coming together in the North Pole East. The virtual runs were all going perfectly; the emails were pouring in over the computer; the elves in the toy shop were working furiously to complete all of the kids' wishes; and the cafeteria was running perfectly, not to mention, deliciously. Orders were pouring in to the Craft Shoppe; the reindeer were preparing for their wonderful evening with Santa; and the sleigh was being superbly fancied up with a fresh coat of paint.

EZE and Hector had become good friends and spent many hours learning from each other. Hector was really happy with his new home for him and Madison. The GERKIN SECURITY CENTER was proudly displayed on his facility. Some of the computer elves decided to work for Hector because they liked that side of the computer system. Keeping Santa's System safe was the objective for everybody.

The town was beautifully decorated, even more elaborately than when they were in the North Pole. Wreaths, bows and holly were everywhere. The train was always available to ride around to get to the other facilities. The train track was as smooth as butter. The town was categorically the prettiest town that ever existed. Santa couldn't be more proud of the elves handling the maintenance, for sure!

Santa called for a virtual town meeting where everybody had their screens up in their facilities. He did this from time-to-time just to get the elves to see him like this. He still held some regular town meetings though as it was always great for everybody to see each other in person.

"HO, HO, HO," shouted Santa. "Hello, all of my wonderful elves! What a great town the North Pole East has become. Thank you all for your hard work in making everything so great. I am happy to say that Christmas Eve is upon us tomorrow, and it's going to be a spectacular night for us. Our System is good to go, so all of the children will be so very happy when they wake up from their good night of sleep." All of the elves shouted joyfully, the music started playing, and everybody started dancing. They all knew that they had done their part to make Christmas the most special day ever!

Santa was ready for his special evening. He dressed in his finest red outfit, and shined his black boots until they were spotless. "Only the best for the children," he said proudly to Mrs. Claus. She looked at him with admiration, and she wished him a safe night and knew everything would go smoothly.

Rudolph was waiting outside the barn, making sure his nose was shined up and ready to go. He knew he had to light the way through the night. He called into the barn for the deer to hurry up and come out. "Santa will be here soon. Is everybody ready?" Rudolph yelled.

They all shouted, "Absolutely – we live for this night!"

EZE and Hector sat proudly in their computer center and watched their reindeer friends get ready for Santa. They could see Santa was on his way to them. The sleigh was all ready to go and loaded up with toys when Santa reached the barn. He called all of his reindeer over and said, "It's time to go!"

"We are ready for you, Santa. Let's do this perfectly!" the reindeer shouted.

Lilly came quietly into the computer center to check on EZE, and sat down by Madison. They both looked lovingly at EZE and Hector, and they were both so very proud. Lilly smiled from one elf ear to the other elf ear! Madison nodded in agreement as she rolled up into a ball on her pillow, the happiest dog ever.

As Santa and his reindeer flew off into the night, it was the most magical night ever. Everything happened just as they planned it, and they knew there would be millions of happy children in the morning! Santa surprised EZE and Hector by putting a camera inside his sleigh. Santa looked over at the camera and said to EZE and Hector, "Please tell your team I couldn't have done this without you! I will see you in the morning!"

"Merry Christmas!"

Santa shouted for all to hear in the
North Pole East.

Made in the USA
Lexington, KY
19 August 2018